Please Let It Snow

*For A. M. B., who knows
about wishes*

PUFFIN BOOKS
Published by the Penguin Group
Penguin Books USA Inc., 375 Hudson Street, New York, New York 10014, U.S.A.
Penguin Books Ltd, 27 Wrights Lane, London W8 5TZ, England
Penguin Books Australia Ltd, Ringwood, Victoria, Australia
Penguin Books Canada Ltd, 10 Alcorn Avenue, Toronto, Ontario, Canada M4V 3B2
Penguin Books (N.Z.) Ltd, 182-190 Wairau Road, Auckland 10, New Zealand
Penguin Books Ltd, Registered Offices: Harmondsworth, Middlesex, England

First published in the United States of America by Viking Penguin Inc., 1989
Simultaneously published by Puffin Books
Published in a Puffin Easy-to-Read edition, 1996

1 3 5 7 9 10 8 6 4 2

Text copyright © Harriet Ziefert, 1989
Illustrations copyright © Amy Aitken, 1989
All rights reserved

Puffin® and Easy-to-Read® are registered trademarks of Penguin Books USA Inc.

THE LIBRARY OF CONGRESS HAS CATALOGED THE PREVIOUS PUFFIN EDITION
UNDER CATALOG CARD NUMBER 88-62145

Puffin Easy-to-Read ISBN 0-14-038294-1
Printed in the United States of America

Reading Level 1.6

Please Let It Snow

Harriet Ziefert
Pictures by Amy Aitken

PUFFIN BOOKS

I have a new snow suit.

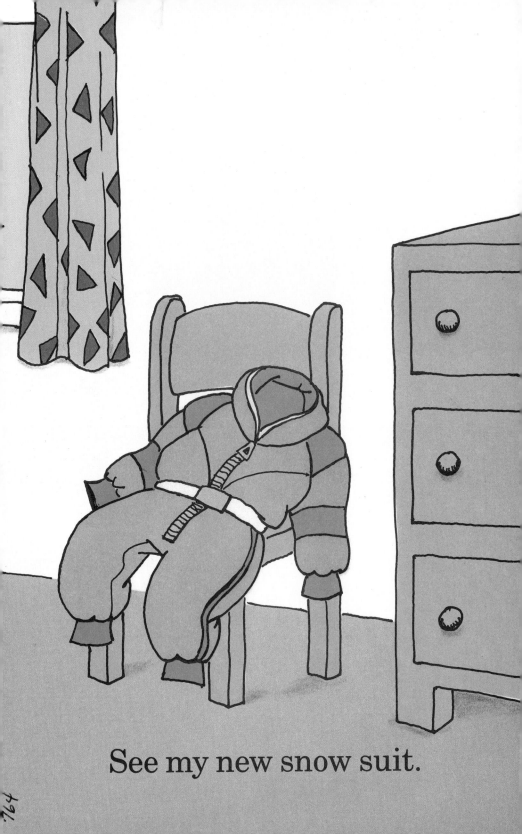

See my new snow suit.

I have a new snow hat.

I have new snow boots.

And I have new mittens.

I wait for snow.

I wait and wait
and wait.
But every day
the sun shines.

In the morning
I run to the window.

I open the shade
and...

the sun is shining!
So I can't wear
my new snow suit.
I can't wear
my new snow hat.

I can't wear
my new snow boots.

And I can't wear
my new mittens.

I get dressed.

But *not* for snow.

Every night I say to myself—
please let it snow...
please let it snow.

But every morning
the sun shines.

I give up!
I stop wishing
for snow.

At night I just
get into bed.

In the morning I do not
even open the shade.

I get dressed.

But *not* for snow.

I walk to the front door
and pull it open.

Guess what?

It snowed!
It *really* snowed!

I put on my new snow suit...

and my new snow hat...

and my new snow boots…

and my new mittens.

See my snow ball!

See my snow angel!

See my snow man!